This book belongs to:

_____

The illustrations were done in watercolor on paper
The text type was set in Founders Caslon
The display type was set in Centaur
Composed in the United States of America
Art Directed by Jennifer Schaber
Designed by Rudy Ramos, Ramos Design Studio
Edited by Erin Murphy
Production Supervised by Lisa Brownfield

Printed in Hong Kong by South Sea International Press Ltd.

www.northlandpub.com

FIRST IMPRESSION
ISBN 0-87358-742-1

Library of Congress Catalog Card Number 99-19711
Cataloging-in-Publication Data
Dengler, Marianna, date.
Fiddlin' Sam / by Marianna Dengler ; illustrated by Sibyl Graber Gerig.
p. cm.
Summary: Wandering through the Ozarks and bringing joy to people
with his music, Fiddlin' Sam seeks the right person to take up his
fiddle and carry on the practice.
ISBN 0-87358-742-1
[1. Violin Fiction. 2. Music Fiction. 3. Ozark Mountains
Fiction.] I. Gerig, Sibyl Graber, ill. II. Title.
PZ7.D4145Fi 1999
[Fic]—dc21   99-19711

0690/7.5M/9-99

Fiddlin' Sam

BY **Marianna Dengler**

ILLUSTRATED BY **Sibyl Graber Gerig**

99
rising moon

A long time ago in the Ozark Mountains, there lived a man called Fiddlin' Sam. He had little to call his own, only the clothes on his back and a fine old lionhead fiddle.

Yet Sam was a happy man. He loved fiddlin'!

Like his pa before him, Sam traveled the back roads, stopping at farms and towns. And he was always welcome.

No matter how busy they were, folks dropped whatever they were doing and gathered 'round. Why? Because when Sam tucked that fiddle under his chin and struck up a tune, something happened.

Something magic.

The folk said Sam had a gift. They said he could fiddle away their worries. He could fiddle away their cares. He could fiddle away the achin' in their bones.

And they'd laugh and clap and tap their toes, and before long they were dancing.

Sam fiddled high, and he fiddled low.

He fiddled fast, and he fiddled slow.

His prancing bow kept the beat.

And afterward, they'd heap his plate with golden brown hush puppies and fragrant possum stew, or cornbread and kidney beans with apple pie. Only the best for the fiddler would do.

It pleasured Sam to fill his belly and share the Ozark news, but when darkness fell he'd take his leave. The folk were always kind to offer him a bed, but, truth to tell, he liked to sleep out under the stars.

Fiddlin' Sam was a happy man, but he never forgot what his pa had said when he was teaching Sam to fiddle. "This ain't a gift, Son. It's a loan. You gotta pass the music along."

The day Sam was headed over to the Hatley place, it was hotter'n blazes. As he trudged along, he was wishing hard for some shade. In fact, he was thinking how good it would feel to dunk his feet in a nice cool crick.

Then he heard the rattler hiss.

He looked down.

The snake lay coiled in the middle of the path. He had almost stepped on it.

Before he could move, the snake struck. It buried its fangs in his leg. Then it slithered away into the bushes.

For a moment Sam just stared at the spot where the snake had been. Then he hobbled over to a log and sank down. His leg was beginning to pain him something fierce.

I'm a goner, he thought. *Sure as shootin'.*

He took the fiddle off his back and looked at the lion's head. The lion's eyes seemed to look straight back at him, and his heart filled up with a terrible sorrow.

If he died, his fine old fiddle would lie here in the sun and the rain and the snow until it was nothing but dust.

The music would die!

What came next was never clear in Sam's mind. A fever raged. He was out of his head. Sometimes he seemed to be walking through fragrant pines, light as air and feeling fine. Other times he'd be crawling down a burning road, parched with thirst, the fiddle dragging along behind.

At last, though, he fell asleep. And he slept and slept and slept.

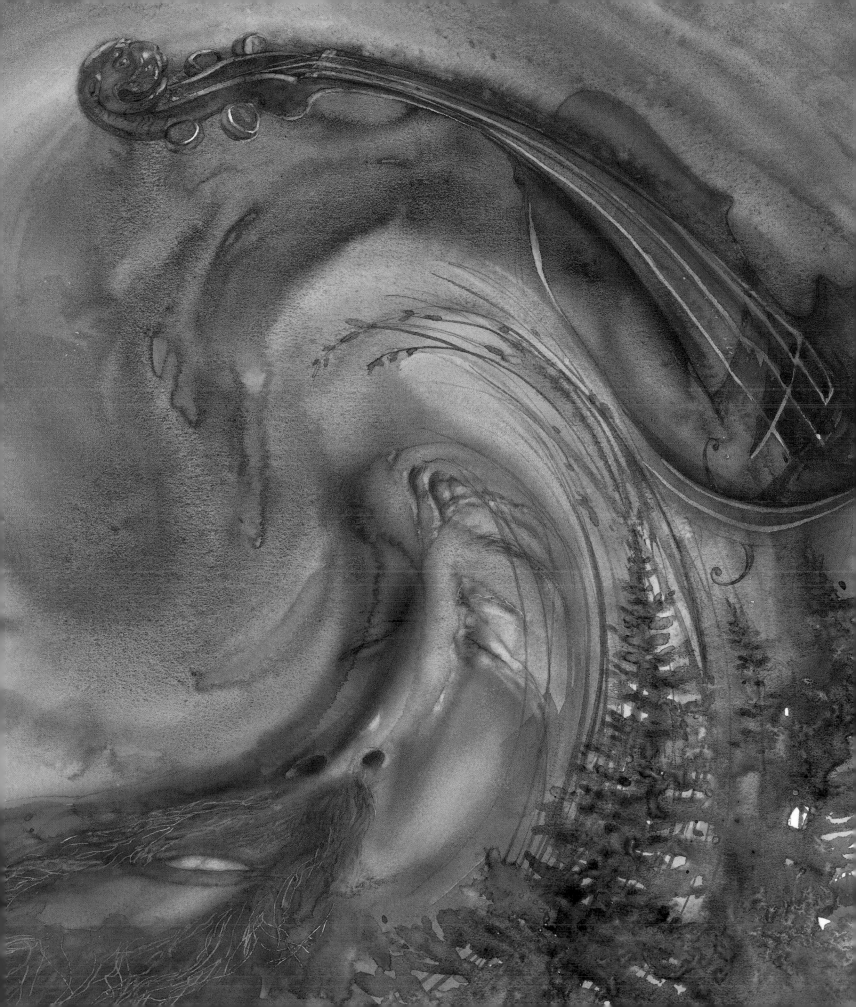

When Sam woke, the air was clean and fresh. Overhead was the prettiest pine tree. A crick gurgled close by.

He blinked, thinking it was a dream, but the pine stayed right where it was.

He sniffed and smelled a campfire.

"I'm alive!" he said, in wonder.

"Yup. Your fever's broke," said the red-headed, freckle-faced young feller who was hunkered down beside him.

Sam looked at him in wonder. "How'd I get here?"

"You ain't heavy," the boy said. "And it ain't far."

"I'm beholden to you," said Sam.

"'Twern't much," said the boy. He was just reaching manhood with whiskers not quite full, but his body was already long and lean and strong.

Sam sat up. Then he saw the fiddle leaning up against the tree. "You brung that too?"

"That's a mighty fine old fiddle," said the boy.

"That it is," said Sam, and his heart was glad.

Sam stayed at the camp in the pine grove for quite a spell. The boy was building a cabin all by himself. It was a big job, and at first Sam could only watch. Later, though, he was able to help. He'd never be able to repay the boy's kindness, but he could see to it that the cabin was snug before the cold weather set in.

And every evening after supper, Sam played the lionhead fiddle.

He was fond of the boy. Maybe it was foolish, but Sam kept hoping that he would be the one. But the boy only listened, tapping his toe in time to the music.

Finally, the old restlessness set in, and Sam knew he had to move on.

The boy knew it, too. "You'll be goin' tomorrow," he said.

"Yup," said Sam. "I gotta."

The boy stared into the fire. His face was sad.

"Come along," Sam suggested. "If'n you do, I'll teach you to fiddle."

"I'd like that," said the boy, "but I got a feel for the land."

"That's so," said Sam, nodding. "Well, you been mighty kind. I ain't never gonna forget."

"You take this with you," said the boy, and he handed Sam the biggest rattlesnake's tail he had ever seen.

"That snake was standin' guard," said the boy. "I had to kill him to get to you."

Sam looked hard at the snake's tail. "Folks say that the snake that keeps a vigil is possessed," he said.

"I heard that," said the boy, "and I also heard that the tail has powers."

"Maybe that's so," Sam said, and he worked the rattle into one of the curly holes in the belly of the fiddle. Then he shook the fiddle.

The snake's tail rattled.

The boy grinned.

Sam grinned back. Then he tucked the fiddle under his chin and began to play.

He fiddled high and low, fast and slow.

His prancing bow kept the beat.

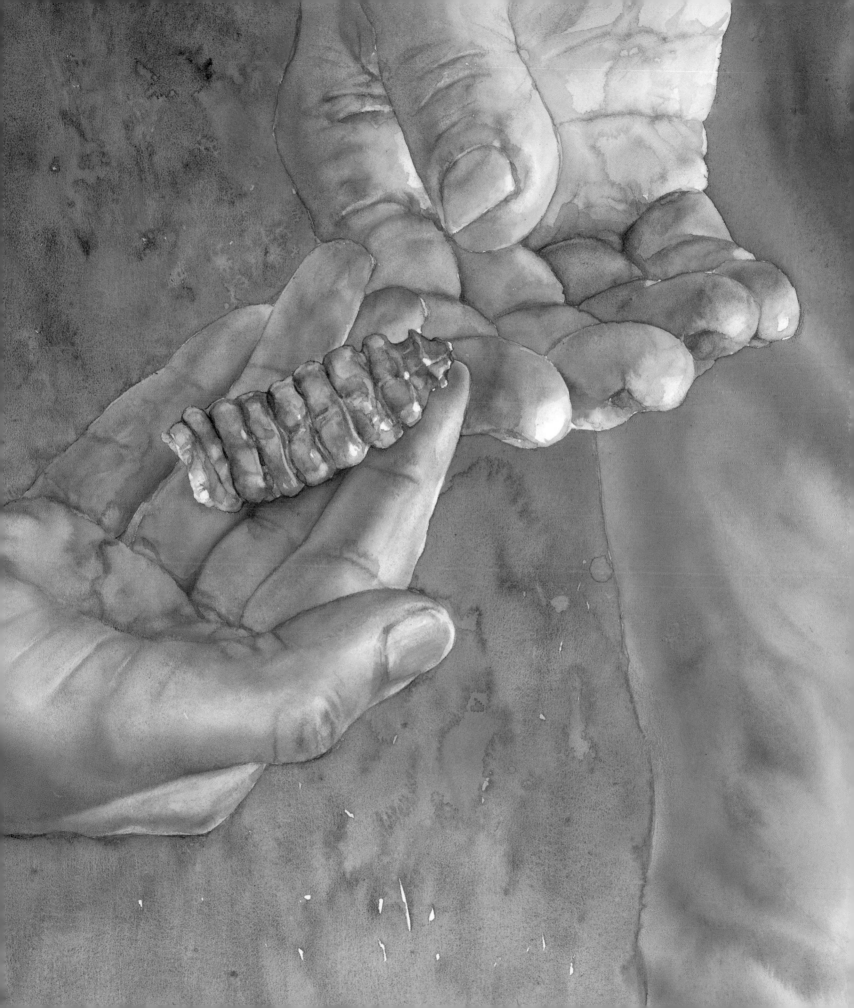

But that night, strange new tunes came to him. Forgetting the boy, forgetting the snake, he fiddled on, long and sweet.

And the single thread of the fiddle tune reached up and up. It mingled with the wind in the pines and meandered on to the sky.

When Sam laid his fiddle down, he saw that the boy was asleep.

The next morning, they said goodbye and Sam went on his way.

He traveled the length and breadth of the Ozarks. And when folks saw him coming down the road, they hollered, "Here comes Fiddlin' Sam!"

And he fiddled fast and slow.

He fiddled high and low.

His prancing bow kept the beat.

Then the music changed, and he fiddled on long and sweet.

And folks all sat down at his feet as the single thread of the fiddle tune reached up and up, mingled with the wind in the pines, and meandered on to the sky.

And folks loved him more and more.

Day after day, Sam fiddled his way from farm to farm and town to town.

One thing was sure. In the Ozarks, crops thrived and folks were content.

Some said it was Sam who brought the good fortune. Some said it was the fiddle. Some said it was the music.

Fiddlin' Sam was a happy man. And there was still time to find someone to take up the fiddle.

The years went by, and there came an aching in Sam's joints that couldn't be fiddled away. More and more he was sleeping in the soft beds folks offered him. More and more he was remembering his pa's words. "This ain't a gift, Son. It's a loan. You gotta pass the music along!"

Maybe tomorrow there'd be someone to take up the fiddle.

One gray afternoon, Sam came to the foot of a hill and stopped to rest. The road ahead was steep and winding. Chill winds howled off the mountain top, and he knew that winter was near.

He sank down by the side of the road. He loved the folk, and he loved fiddlin', but he was weary and he was old.

All these years he'd tried to find someone to take up the fiddle, but there was no one.

Sam just sat there feeling sick at heart. He couldn't find the strength to even stand up, let alone walk on down the dusty road.

That's when a boy came trudging along, dragging his feet. The boy's clothes were in rags, but under the dust and grime, his hair was red and his face was freckled.

"Hey," said Sam and nodded a welcome.

"Hey," said the boy and sat down next to him.

The boy looked familiar, but Sam couldn't figure why.

"Where you headed, Son?" Sam asked.

"Home," the boy said.

"Where's that?"

"South of here," the boy said. "Down near the Hatley place."

Sam stared at the boy with the red hair and the freckled face, and things commenced to come together. In his mind he was seeing another red-haired boy, one he'd known a long time ago, one he'd been right fond of. That other boy was building a cabin in the pines because he had a feel for the land.

Father and son? Had to be. This boy sitting here next to him was a ringer for that other boy.

"Son of a gun!" said Sam.

"You headin' down toward the Hatley place, too?" the boy asked. "All that long way?"

"Happens, I am," he said.

Then he got to his feet and clapped the boy on the shoulder. "Come on," he said, and they headed on down the road, together.

That evening, they stopped in a glen, and the boy built a fire while the old man rested. Sam shared his meal with the hungry boy who told about being restless on his pa's farm.

"So I left," he said, "and I been up and down the Ozarks lookin' for somethin' better." He studied the ground. "Now I gotta go back and tell him I ain't found it."

Sam listened hard to the boy. Then, without a word, he took out his fiddle and began to play.

He fiddled fast, and he fiddled slow.

He fiddled high, and he fiddled low.

His prancing bow kept the beat.

And the boy hunkered down beside him, listening.

The next morning, nothing was said between them, but they went on together. And that night after supper, Sam played the fiddle again.

This time he saw what he'd been looking for. The boy's fingers were moving. His hands itched to try the fiddle.

Sam handed it to him and leaned back against a tree, watching.

The boy's eyes lit up as he took the fiddle, but the consarned thing wouldn't stay in his hands.

Sam gave the boy a few pointers, but all he could manage were some awful squeaks and squawks.

Sam chuckled. "You'll get the hang of it," he said.

"Naw," said the boy, "It's a mean old thing!" And he gave Sam back the fiddle.

The next day, and the next, and the one after that, they walked the dusty road.

At last, they came to a farm.

When the folks saw them coming, they hollered, "Here comes Fiddlin' Sam!" Just like they always did.

So Sam tucked the fiddle under his chin and struck up a tune.

After Sam finished playing, he and the boy were treated to a meal they'd not soon forget, and when they went on down the road, they had fresh loaves of bread and chunks of beef in their pockets and warm shawls over their backs.

"You've a mighty fine gift," said the boy.

" 'Tain't a gift," said Sam. "It's a loan. I gotta pass it along."

The weather grew more chill. Each step for the old fiddler was pain. But with the boy's strong shoulder to lean on, he struggled along toward the cabin in the pine grove.

In the evenings by the fire, the boy fooled around with the fiddle. And danged if that fiddle wasn't starting to sing.

If only I have time, Sam thought. *If only I have time!*

One night, the old man lay in his shawl, shivering with cold. His limbs ached something fierce, but he was watching the boy play the lionhead fiddle. The boy's face was happy!

Warmth seeped into the old man's heart and spread itself.

The boy was fiddling high and low, then fast and slow. His prancing bow kept the beat. Then he was fiddling long and sweet.

The old man's soul drifted on the fiddle tune—up and up. It mingled with the wind in the pines and meandered on to the sky.

The first flakes of snow were falling when the boy laid the
fiddle down.

"Maybe I could take up the fiddle," he said, gazing into the fire.
"What do you think?"

No answer.

The boy looked down. Then his eyes filled with tears. The old
fiddler could no longer hear him.

The next morning, the boy buried the old man under a pine.

"Rest easy, Sam," he said.

Then he took up the fiddle and went on.

That night, at the cabin in the pine grove near the Hatley place, a man watched his son play a lionhead fiddle. His heart was glad, for at last the boy's eyes shone with pleasure.

The music took the father back to a year when times were hard. He remembered a man, a fiddle, and a snake standing guard. Could this be the same fiddle? Was there a rattlesnake's tail in its belly?

When the son put the fiddle down the father picked it up and shook it. The snake's tail rattled.

"Sam," he said. "Sam."

Still today, a fiddler travels the length and breadth of the Ozarks, stopping at farms and towns. When folks see him coming down the road, they drop what they're doing and gather 'round.

And he fiddles away their worries. He fiddles away their cares. He fiddles away the achin' in their bones.

He fiddles high, and he fiddles low.

He fiddles fast, and he fiddles slow.

His prancing bow keeps the beat.

Then he fiddles long and sweet.

And folks all sit down at his feet, while the single thread of the fiddle tune reaches up and up, mingles with the wind in the pines and meanders on to the sky.

To the memory of

SAM HATLEY,

who played the lionhead fiddle
and put the rattlesnake's tail in its belly . . .

To the memory of my father,
who took up the fiddle and the promise . . .

To my daughters,
who hold the music in trust . . .

And to all who come after.
— M. D.

To Winston, with love.
— S. G. G.

juv.   00-981
D   Dengler, Marianna
                Fiddlin' Sam.

DATE DUE

SE 29 '00			
AP 16 '01			
AP 23 '01			
MY 15 01			
JY 17 01			